Words to Know Before You Read

Let's Learn The Ll Sound

lake
leaps
leash
leave
let
lie
light
little

live
log
long
look
love
lunch
lynx

S0-AGK-818

www.rourkeeducationalmedia.com

Edited by Luana Mitten
Illustrated by Marc Mones
Art Direction, Cover and Page Layout by Tara Raymo

Library of Congress PCN Data

The Lake Mistake / Precious McKenzie
ISBN 978-1-62169-254-6 (hard cover) (alk. paper)
ISBN 978-1-62169-212-6 (soft cover)
Library of Congress Control Number: 2012952750

Rourke Educational Media
Printed in the United States of America,
North Mankato, Minnesota

rourkeeducationalmedia.com

customerservice@rourkeeducationalmedia.com • PO Box 643328 Vero Beach, Florida 32964

THE LAKE MISTAKE

Counselor
Lou

Counselor
Nico

Marcos

Viv

Lani

Will

Written By Precious McKenzie

Illustrated By Marc Mones

"Let's go to the lake," says Counselor Lou.

"Take the picnic lunch," says Counselor Nico.

WILDCAT LAKE

5

"Look at the lake!" sighs Marcos.

"I love it," says Viv.

"I could live here forever," says Will.

The counselors set up the picnic lunch.

Everyone loves the lunch!

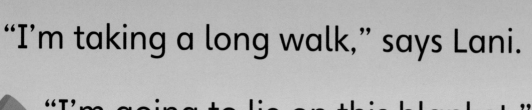

"I'm taking a long walk," says Lani.

"I'm going to lie on this blanket," says Marcos.

"I'm going to sit on this log and read a book," says Viv.

Lani and Will walk along the lake.

"Do you hear that noise?" asks Will.

"Look around that log," says Lani.
They find nothing there.

"Shine your light over there," says Lani.

Will shines his light under the low branches.

"Can you see it?" asks Lani.

14

"Look! A little kitten!" whispers Will.

"Let's make a leash and take her back to the lake," says Lani.

"Look at the cute kitten we found," says Lani.

The kitten let out a low growl.

"Let it go! Let it go!" shouts Counselor Lou.

The kitten leaps for Will's leg.

"That is not a kitten! That is a lynx! A wild cat!" yells Viv.

"Leave it alone! And RUN!" shouts Counselor Lou.

After Reading Word Study

Picture Glossary

Directions: Look at each picture and read the definition. Write a list of all of the words you know that start with the same sound as *love*. Remember to look in the book for more words.

lake (LAKE): A lake is a large body of fresh water that is surrounded by land.

lie (LYE): When you lie down you are stretched out, usually on your back, stomach, or side.